She is Me

Wick'D Love

ISBN: 0999568323
ISBN-13:978-0-9995683-2-3

DEDICATION

This book is dedicated to every reader who dared to pick this book up and read it from beginning to end. We ask that you continue to dream big, think outside of the box, and not worry about fitting in, any place other than within. Walk in your divine light, no matter who judges you. Dare to be different — Dare to be you.

CONTENTS

Introduction

Traditionally a books intro would tell you about the main text; however, Wick'D Love is a totally different Beast and defies the norms of tradition for various reasons; with the primal reason being that: tradition is meant to lock you in a continued state of thinking. Thinking that typically benefits others more than it actually benefits you, and your Divine Spirit; that resides within (also referenced as your intuition or God).

Our misalignment with this "Divine Spirit or God," is the reason for your pain, frustration, money, relationship problems and anything else that you can put on thee: "I have the right to complain because" list.

Today Wick'D Love dares you to defy the tradition and start to believe in you, as much as you believe in others; but more than: *Revelations*. We dare you to follow your intuition and put forth energy in connecting your mind with your spirit, and finding the balance required to endure such everlasting Euphoria; as you build your: *Kingdom*.

We dare you to focus inward, and push out all distractions that keep you from answering questions like: "What truly makes me happy? Why am I not, in that happy place? Who's keeping me from getting there? How do I get there?", and other simple questions that require: *Acknowledgement* — before you can answer honestly.

Allow those emotions to consume you and stand strong in your: *Reflections;* to face them. Only there will you find your true-self, and start the process of connecting and growing, in a way that you would have never previously imagined, while under the influence of "tradition."

When wearing proper eyes — there in the light of truth; will you find: *Deliverance* and infinite, Divine answers to questions like: "What is lifes' purpose? What is my purpose? What was I meant to do?"

Allow: *Perseverance* to fuel your passion and your intuition to be your guide.

EXPECTATIONS

Elations is to be expected. Wick'D Love is going to take you on a journey sharing our happiness, love and vitality. We will challenge the norm, and dare you to think outside of the box-o-tradition, while understanding that it's okay to be excited about who you are, and to also understand that; you have the right to not fear what others may say and/or think about you. After all... I'm sure that your Divine purpose was not to be tongue lashed by others who disapprove of your very existence, and want you to conform to their way of thinking: just so they won't be forced to look at their own reflection in the mirror, and acknowledge its existence and all that it unveils. Self-accountability and responsibility is a high power, that most fear and fear is the true root of all evil.

WHY

Wick'D Love writes in the manner that we do because we want to take you on a journey. We want to tell-a-tale that opens your mind and allows practical-logic and endless possibilities to flow. We want you to know and understand your worth — no matter how much doubt and darkness may surround you. When you are whole; your Divine: *Synergy* is strong, and there is no force that can penetrate you. We want you to know that failure is a part of success and that it's okay to fail if you need to: as all great masters do. We write because we want you to love, forgive, and accept all of you; changing only the things that you don't like about the darker aspects of who you are (as judged by only you of course), while continuously growing, challenging, and nurturing all others.

KINGDOM

Kat's moans echo throughout the house. Her energy overpowering the air in the room; leaving you to consume all that she is. The crystal chandelier shakes below. Beautiful, mystical and whimsical, describes the sound permeating throughout, as Mona's hand's intimately slides up Kat's thighs, while my tongue caresses her soft temples. The curves of her nipples run parallel with my tongue, as it wraps around the entire areola and slowly works back and forth: back and forth, in a repetitive and consistent motion. They instantly firm, enticing me to suck even harder.

Mona caressing Kat's body while leaving a trail of flummoxed nerves as rich, velvety-silk, kream; cascades across my fingers and makes its way down her thighs. Mona's hands glide down the verge of her stomach, rendering Kat: powerless to her touch. My fingers make a circle on the inner thigh of her leg where she is overly sensitive, causing her to squirm and moan louder and louder, with intense pleasure and excitement. Like the end of Flower Duet; I grow excited, yet sad. I can feel her swelling, as her soft ripples start to form around me. Kat can't resist being touched in particular spots, without giving in to me. We kum together and I swiftly pull out. She showers us with her sweet-love; reminding me of her delicious peach cobbler and the way the slippery peaches slide around your mouth, just before coating your throat with its warm, silky, sweet, sticky, residue. She loves the taste of Kat; just as much as I do.

Her body goes calm after being overwhelmed with intense excitement, joy, and wonderful pleasure. She gives in, and allows all of the feelings and sensations to flow through; what she describes as: "good pain"; leaving her body in a complete stage of euphoric-stasis: as she enjoys her high.

Mona sits up, face saturated with Kat's kream; as she gazes at me with those begging eyes. Fingers sticky and sweet, she stops my hands from rubbing on Kat; and places them on her face instead. I begin to rub it in as she closes her eyes, ravishing in the moment. I kiss her lips; still sticky and sweet. Her body now covered in goose bumps, as my hand glides down her cheek, followed by my lips whispering softly against her sweet skin: 'who's pussy is this?' I reach her neck, just under the ear, when I hear a sultry moan coming from Mona. The harder I suck, the more she squirms. She releases another moan; that was not neck sucking worthy and her body shook. I smile instantly with a somewhat lush and malevolent grin. I would love to take credit but that could only mean one thing. I glance over my shoulder and there was Kat, ready to play. Her fingers already deep inside of Mona; causing her entire body to arch – as hers just did. Kat loves caressing the G-spot in a slow and torturous motion; that's both exciting, and nerve rattling; making her entire body feel as though it's going to explode from parlous satisfaction and pleasure. 'I love it when my Queens' squirt.' – I think, to myself.

I play with Mona's nipples, while Kat works her magic… I slowly apply more pressure, mixed with a bit of pain – to her nipples, as Kat consistently works on unlocking Pandora's Box. The feeling is currently beyond earth shattering for Mona. Her nipples hard; leaving her entire body quivering in pure pleasure. Her body convulses and her moans grow louder and more rapid. 'She'll be here any moment now.' – I think to myself. I pull her hair, making her back arch and draw her body closer to mine; bracing her as she kums, allowing her to reach her complete, erotic-climax. Sheets completely saturated; I give my hand to each of the ladies, helping them off of the bed one-by-one. Kat extends her hands and caresses my head, in a manner that only she can.

Mona is already nibbling on my earlobe and kisses her way down to my chest. She moves slowly allowing her soft and perky, lips to touch every inch of my body as she loves on me with grace and pleasure. My body: filled with continuous balls of energy, moving so fast, that it makes me feel as though I'm going to explode. My dick grows harder, and my body just turned into a ball of nerves.

I look to my right and there was Kat – licking every inch of me. She eases her way down to my lower abdomen, with Mona following her lead. Kat loves to flick her tongue back and forth between the creases of my legs. Teasing me, she commands her tongue to my inner thigh; using it to create a figure eight. 'A little payback'; I think out loud. Kat ascends while continuously creating figure eights with her tongue, making me want to knut all over her face. Mona grabs My Love Stick and starts to nurture it very softly, caressing it up and down; while spitting on it. The combined sensation of: great head, offered by two beautiful goddesses consumes me. They sense me holding back and fighting the temptation of their magic. "So naughty" Kat whispers in my ear – just before they both push me, making me fall onto the bed. There's a slight chill across the silky sheets; mimicking the crisp nights air floating in through the, nano-scale opening in the window. I flinch while trying to escape the cold, when I notice that I can't move my right arm. Soon after followed the restraint of my left arm too. My Queens' are being really mischievous right now – which usually means I get to spank them later. They pin me down and leave hickeys all over my body, in a parallel and synchronized motion, triggering all of my nerves; while heightening all of my senses. The sensation causes a feeling that's indescribable. It's both painful, but oh so magical at the same time: The satisfaction of the release, as my knut lands on both of my Queens, covering their bodies from head to toe. They smile simultaneously as they enjoy massaging my kream into each other's bodies'. They kiss, cleaning some residual kum from their lips.

I ease out of the bed, joining the ladies and lead them to the bathroom where we all bathe. Feeling guilty from all of the mess that I just caused, I washed each of them individually; while the other patiently waited their turn. Kat goes first as Mona gets playful and rubs soap all over me. Growing more anxious and out of control, Mona attempts to assist me in bathing Kat: against my wishes. I smack her on her soft, wet, ass; letting her know that she's misbehaving. It looks like she enjoyed that more than I wanted her to. Repeatedly disobeying me, she continues her attempts. Kat absolutely hates it when her bath time is interrupted. She's very particular about things. Kat looks at Mona and gives off an expression of caution, much like a cat hissing at another, but did so with an opulent smile. I still marvel at this unspoken language that they speak. Mona doesn't take heed so I smack her on the ass so loud that it echo's in the shower. That one had to sting a bit. As a consequence, for being disobedient, I make her get down on her knees in the shower and wait her turn. Kat exits the bath into the shower. The water runs off of our bodies, onto hers. I signal Mona, and she slowly crawls over, and sits in front of Kat, who's basking under the waterfall of the shower.

I stand back and watch. The view reflecting like a beautiful, work of art, as water cascades down Kat's body, perfectly hugging every curve as if they were fated to intertwine: Continuously flowing down her silhouetted curves; joining back together at the tip of the clitoris; as the water flows from above. The water splashes onto Mona's face, as she enjoys her repercussions. Kat squirts, leaving Mona painted in Kat's energy. She immediately turns to Daddy; tongued curled while in motion. With naturalness; I stick my dick in her mouth, and she latches on immediately. I force her head making sure that she takes all of me. We grind in a synchronized motion, as she makes a complete mess of herself while slurping every drop.

We exit the shower; all clean and rejuvenated. Mona turns to Kat and dries her body from head to toe. She loves touching her, and does so whenever she can. Kat walks over to me and dries the side of my face with the towel. She gazes, as the water slowly, rolls downward to the small of my back. Extending my arms above my head, she dries my torso; working her way down to my lower extremities. I turn, and Mona's spraying some body oil that she picked up from this women empowerment party; all over Kat's body.

Completely dry and ready for some excitement, we make our way into the closet. We are all very excited for this cruise, and in desperate need of a tri-cation. We get dressed and I pack some last-minute items into our bags; as the Queens' are consulting one another for fashion advice. I love watching the two of them together. I sit back on the couch and start to admire my beautiful Queens, when suddenly the

doorbell rings. It's the car service. 'Ladies, we have to go!
The car is here' I yell. They rush out the door leaving us
gentlemen literally holding all of the bags. The driver looks
at me and we have a silent brah moment. After too long a
duration filled with complete and awkward silence; I just
smile and shake my head. I can only imagine all the things
that are running through his head right now. I put my
sunglasses on, turned and grabbed my bags from the ground;
leading the way to the car. The driver grabbed the remaining
bags and eventually followed.

We arrive at the car where the Queens' are standing and
waiting. They dare not open the car door, so they've patiently
waited for me. 'Good Girls' I utter, as I approach and open
the door for them. After closing the door; I turn, and there
was the driver: his lips within locking distance from mine;
so, a natural reaction for me, was to step back.

I give him the strangest stare while trying to figure out: 'why
in the hell he's standing this close to me?' He stared at me
with extreme aversion and zeal. I pull my glasses down and
step towards the car; as he moves closer, to open the door
for me. Door slamming behind me as I step in and turn to

glance out of the window; just in time to see him slap his forehead in contempt. The driver finally enters the car and we take off. Traffic was light, although our city has become over crowded – given the massive amounts of people, who now move here regularly. We just hope to make it safely, considering that the majority are unmindfully high.

REVELATIONS

I pull out my J3K or Jameson 3000, leaving myself a voice reminder to dig deeper for opportunity. We arrive at the airport two hours early: as always. We check our bags and head for the nearest VIP member lounge. "This is great. It allows for all of us to get caught up on some work or just chill-lax." Mona says. We enter the lounge, and Kat scans her ticket after being greeted by the associate behind the desk. You hear the *beep* and the associate looks at Kat, then looks back and forth between her screen and Kat's beautiful; but currently agitated face. She does this at least three times. "Mrs. Bordeaux, I see that you are traveling with a guest today." Kat smiles, turns to Mona and says: "Babe she needs your boarding pass." The associate then turns and looks at Mona and Kat with that same back and forth motion, like she's putting a Jenga puzzle together in her head, and is rapidly confused. Mona extends her arm, and delivers her phone to Paula. "Here you are…Paula." Mona says, after taking a brief pause and looking at her name tag, to confirm her name. Paula takes the phone and scans Mona in. She hands Mona her phone back with certain haste, as though her phone had cooties or something. Paula turns and looks in my direction stating: "I can help the next guest please." I walk up to the desk, as the Queens' remain standing; waiting for me to scan through. I catch Paula glaring at Kat and Mona through her peripheral. She's looking as though they are an aberration to the female species. Paula turns to me: "boarding pass please. I mean: Good Morning, sir. May I please scan your boarding pass?" she asks: with a smile. I hand Paula my phone. She stares at the screen, as my profile pops up. "Ah–Mr. Bordeaux." she says, as her smile dissipates – upon quickly realizing that Kat and I share the same last name. There's that look sprawled across Paula's face again. The look of complete and utter-uncertainty: a slight abyssal stare.

Paula's disgust eventually dissipates from her face. She shrugged her shoulder and handed me the phone back. She probably thought that we were brother and sister and that Kat was lesbian or something of that nature. She concludes with: "Mr. Bordeaux, please enjoy your time with us, and let us know if there is anything that you need." "Babe, is there anything that you need?" Kat asks Mona. Mona smiles and rubs her hand gently down the side of Kat's face, responding: "No love." She then turns to me; looks and says: "Daddy… is there anything else that you need at the moment?" "No mama – but thank you." I reply. There's that look sprawled across Paula's face – once again: a look of complete, and utter confusion. Paula's mouth drops, and she literally speechless: and I didn't think that this was possible. She's now starring at all three of us with mass confusion. So much so; that Darlene-her co-worker eventually steps in and says: "Mr. and Mrs. Bordeaux, please let me know if there is anything that we can do for you and your guest, during your time with us. Please enjoy and safe travels."

I lead the Queens' by placing my hand on Mona's back as we walk away. With Kat leading the caravan; we enter the lounge and immediately find a place to sit. The ladies are already heading toward the window seats. They sit on the same side, but opposite of me. I continue to stand; ensuring that my Queens' are seated first, and then secure their belongings in the chair next to me. I take my seat, picking up the paper laying on the table, and check out the global news and stocks. I cross my legs and ask the ladies if they would like to grab something to snack on. "Ladies first, I'll be here when you get back." I say, as I smile.

"Can you believe Paula – what's her face?" Mona asks, Kat. "Unfortunately, I can." Kat replies. "Here is the thing. Most people who turn their noses up, are not sure of what is going on, or how to perceive what they are actually seeing. Unfortunately, society has taught them to view what they've just witnessed, and everything else that is not considered the *'norm'* in a certain negative connotation. It further goes on to say that, if you don't view things the way that I say you should, and expect you to; that you're considered a traitor, and not accepted by 'us': the masses. In essence, it's training them how to hate, and my advice is; follow your intuition, stay focused and believe in you. You'll elevate high in life; fulfilling your divine purpose vs. staying stuck in a continuous, repetitive-cycle of misery and self-destruction" Kat concludes. "Wow... so deep and so true." – Mona replies, as she stares at Kat in the most alluring way: almost as if she's fallen in love with her all over again.

I smile in witness of such a beautiful moment that's all mine; as I watch them walk away. 'What a blessing.' – I think to myself. I stare out the window; watching the rainfall, and the planes move about. I'm taking a mental run through my plans for the rest of the day – ensuring that I didn't miss a step: 'Flowers: check; chocolate covered strawberries: check; rose petals: check; sexy lingerie: check; room service: check;

remote-controlled; luminous candles: check; silk-Japanese Bondage Ropes: check. Last – but not least; playlist: check.'. I snap out of it; as the ladies' reproach. Kat hands me a glass filled with yogurt; made up like a parfait, and Mona hands me a plate filled with strawberries, cheese, nuts and crackers. I sit them on the table next to me. 'Queens' – I say; as I slightly bow my head, to greet them with my: 'thank you'. After a while; notification came over the intercom calling the next planes, location, destination and gates; that are boarding within the next fifteen minutes. Our flight was amongst this group, so we packed up and got ready to head over to Gate "C34".

We exit the lounge and hop in the all-black, leather, VIP-cart; designated to take VIP clients to their respective gates. As soon as we arrive to the gate, we are escorted directly to first class; as though there were trying to shield us from the paparazzi or something. I gather our bags and place them in the overhead bin, and take my seat, joining the ladies. Mona is in between Kat and I, and already talking about how she's: "ready to recline her seat and go straight to sleep" quote-on-quote. I smile, tickled at how cozy she's already gotten. I can understand why though: we've had a pretty *intense* twenty-four hours. After last night, and again-this morning. I'm considering going to sleep too. Kat seconds that; but will most likely stay up and read while the two of us sleeps.

Mona reclines her seat preparing to sleep for a bit. "Mr. and Mrs. Bordeaux?" – the stewardess's tone asked in question; in efforts of properly identifying us. "Can I get either of you anything before take-off?" she asks. We place our orders, with Kat ordering a: "Vodka and Cranberry"; while I ordered a: 'Classic Mojito with extra lime'. "And for your daughter?" Kelly asked. "Would she like something to drink?" 'Oh, this is going to be good.' – I think to myself: as I chuckle a bit. Kat turns to Mona; places one hand on her, and gives her a little shake. "Babe; what would you like to drink?" Kat asks. "Vodka-Cranberry"; she mumbled reluctantly from under the covers. Kelly's slightly muddle by what she just heard. From my view, it looks like she was a bit excited as well. "I really wanted to order her to go. She has me so wet right now, and she's really cute too." Kat text to me. I chuckle; as I read the message on my phone. 'Oh – great minds; My Love: great minds' I typed in response. When she asked if she could get us anything; I almost said: "I'll have you in my suite tonight." – Kat replied; followed by: "Did you see those

Girls? So wet right now…" reads her reply. I respond with an *emoji*; smiling back. 'I'll take care of you later My Love. No worries.' I send back with the *kitty cat* – emoji and a smile. Kat responds with a: "waterfall, blush and smile": emoji.

Kelly returns with our drinks, and we quickly put our phones away; like little kids busted doing something wrong. It was actually quite comical. We grab the drinks. Kelly started to pass me my drink first, and I reject it stating: 'ladies first, please.' She then arched her body across my seat; to hand Kat her drink. Her breasts were even more prevalent now, than before. 'Did she change bras?'; I wondered to myself. Kelly was so close, that her breast actually brushed the side of my cheek. Her skin was soft and smooth – like silk. She takes a step back and proceeds in handing Kat – Mona's drink as well; leaving her to have to reach over me once again. This time, both breasts ended up in my face; as Kelly braced herself on the back of the seat; in efforts to deliver this last drink to Kat. "You smell really good. May I ask what you're wearing?" Kat responds, in that sweet and seductive tone that no one can resist. "It's called: *Flirt!*" – Kelly replies; as she smiles at Kat, with a familiar alluring response. "Yes: you are." Kat responds in a sultry, yet calm voice; as she smiles at her. Kelly retreats, just as Mona is starting to incline into upright position. I can still smell the reminisce of her perfume lingering, as she turns to walk away.

Mona in full position; witnesses me starring at Kelly, as she switches from side-to-side; back to her station. She takes a sip from her drink and joins me in wonder. After she is no longer in sight, she kisses me softly on my lips stating: "She'll never be able to satisfy you the way that I do." I smile as our lips part from one another; biting me before she goes back to sipping on her Vodka and Cranberry. Mona then turns to Kat and slowly moves her hand under the cover, and up her skirt. She moves her thongs to the side, and finds that Kat is already very wet. Mona smiles, presses the power button on the vibrator, and inconspicuously slips her middle finger into Kat's pussy. Mona motions in and out a few times, ultimately using the vibrations to make her kum. Trying not to make a scene; she pulls out slowly, and uses the same finger to stir her drink; after dropping the vibrator in her glass – where it continues to vibrate and clank against the ice and glass within. Mona then takes that same finger and puts it in her mouth; securing her lips tightly, creating a suction, as she pulls it out. Mona takes another sip before sitting back in her seat: "A girl can't even take a nap without having to worry about someone trying to steal you-two." she comments before she turns, to go back to sleep. Kat and I look at each other and smile. We raise our glasses at the exact same time in a silent toast. Each of us knowing exactly what the other was thinking.

We finish our drinks and handed the glasses to the stewardess, who's waiting to take them prior to lift-off. The plane is moving, and the captain just asked that we all take our seats, and the *fasten seat belt* light came on shortly after. Once cleared, Kat and I reclined into sleep position; joining Mona and catching up on some much-needed rest.

ACKNOWLEDGEMENT

San Juan, Puerto Rico… "I Would have never imagined that there were slot machines in the airports. Vegas: Yes; but Puerto Rico… not so much. This is great." – Mona says; as the luggage immediately drops. We grab our luggage and head to the Concierge. He pulls a car to take the three of us to the Port. "I love what the culture represents and all of the potential here in Puerto Rico." I say.

We arrive at the Port. Kat is pulling out all of the paper work needed to board. We have priority boarding, so a gentleman – concierge assigned to us takes the paperwork from Kat, and were immediately brought to our suite, where the ladies drop their purses. I pop the champagne, as Kat taste the chocolate-covered strawberries and Mona opens the large seamless glass doors; leading to the massive balcony. I sip and admire the waters from the middle of the room; sun shining bright, creating a glow that is simply magical; especially when reflective off of Kat's beautiful caramel-toned skin. "It's nice being a VIP member." Mona says with her feet curled underneath her body, as she sits in a Yoga pose across the white couch; while the butler bows to offer her a glass of wine. Kat and I take our glasses from Henry as well, and we prepare for a toast. 'Here's to a fun filled, memorable, sexy, kick-ass, 'trication' – I say; as we sip. The doorbell chimes: *ding-dong* "Must be the bags." Kat says. Henry answers – and has the bags brought into the suite. Our itineraries and excursions are found sitting on the overly-humongous, center table; that graces the suite with its presence; as you walk.

They curve with the table in a fan-style; complementing its flawless craftsmanship. Henry takes the bags up-to the bedroom. He starts to unpack and puts the clothes away. We head to the VIP lounge to get a bite to eat and explore on our own a bit. The spread looks fattening and delightful. Mona is completely over joyed because she loves to eat. Both ladies love to try new and eclectic things. I head straight for the seafood: It's a buffet forged for a King.

Kat looks for all things pescatarian; as she drifts off checking out the very classy spread. I hear Kat's voice in the near distance, and she sounds disturbed. I turn and look: A waitress bumped into her. "I am so, sorry." – She kept apologizing to Kat. Apparently… she spilled, a little lemon-butter on her shirt. You could tell that she was so embarrassed about it all. She kept asking Kat: "Is there anything I could do to make it up to you?" Kat repeatedly said: "No worries, it's okay, I'll take care of it." Kat then stopped and asked the waitress if she were okay. "Yes I am." the waitress replied. "Thank you for asking." The two lock eyes. Raquel stares at Kat with admiration and attraction. It's that moment when you see something so beautiful that it took your breath away; kind of stare. "Once again, I'm so sorry. I'm more than happy to clean it for you, and drop it off to your room." – Raquel continues. "No thank you, but thank you." Kat replies. "Kat, was it?" she asked in a plighted tone. "Yes – Kat, that's correct." She replied. "Well Kat, I'm Raquel, and it would be my absolute pleasure and honor to clean that stain off of your shirt, and personally return it to you." Raquel says, with a smile, as she brushed the stain with a napkin, that she pulled from the pocket of her apron. "Really, it's no worries." Kat replied, while blushing. "Henry will take care of it for me, but I greatly appreciate your offer." "Everything okay love?" I ask as, I approach the two. "Yes, I'm okay." Kat replies. "Babe: is everything okay?" Mona asks, as she approaches from directly behind me. "Yes, I'm fine." Kat replies in an almost sui-generis tone. "Raquel, this is my husband and our girlfriend Mona." – Kat explains in a very confident and urbane tone: one that may have taken

Raquel by surmise. She appears to be a bit blushed and instantly shy all of a sudden. "Nice to meet you both." Raquel replies, followed by a passive bashful wave. "Well Kat, it was nice bumping into you, hope to see you around." – Raquel says in closing as she walks off. "Have a great rest of your day." – she includes. Although this is one of Kat's favorite shirts; she wasn't worried about the stain. She knew that Henry could get it out, no matter how long it had sat. If not, she would just purchase a new one; which she will most likely do anyway. Kat's lack of negative emotional response to the situation left Mona feeling some type of way. Mona instantly became jealous and felt a bit insecure.

We find our reserved seating near the window. "They should find better help to work in the VIP lounge" – Mona says. Kat and I glance up at each other, then at Mona in a tandem motion. "Not impressed with the lounge?" Kat asks Mona. "It's okay. I just think that people should be more cognizant of their surroundings, and be more careful. Do you know what it will take to get that stain out?" Mona asked with excitement, and what sounded like a bit of frustration too. 'This can't be about lemon butter sauce.' – I think to myself. "Hmm, can I assume that you are referring to Raquel?" Kat asked in a passive and question like tone. "Yes." – Mona responds excitedly. Kat smiles and shakes her head, just before posing the question of: "What would you have done differently in her situation?" she asks Mona. "Well…Um… hmm. Well-I would have made sure that no one was around before I busted through the door, that's for sure" Mona recites. "How do you know that she didn't?" – Kat asks. "Well… Um… hmmm… I guess – I guess; I don't." Mona replies with a bit of a stutter and hesitation. "Is there something that you would like to talk about love?" Kat asked Mona, leaving the floor open for Mona to express any difficult or different types of emotions that she's feeling right now. "No. I guess I'm okay. Maybe I was being a bit ridiculous and judgmental too." Mona admitted. "No worries." Kat says. "Happens to the best of us. Try to stay focused though love. If you don't control yourself, then everyone will" – Kat says; while covering Mona's hand with hers. "You're absolutely right. Thanks for the reminder." Mona replies. She then turns and looks at us both. "I'm really sorry if I made a scene or appeared foolish at the very least." Mona expressed. Kat and I both smile at her, and we finish our meal.

We head back to the room. The Queens' need to shower, change clothes and I have a bit of work to do. I give Henry Kat's shirt, and ask that he have the stain removed before returning it. I log in and check some emails. There are a few acquisitions that we're trying to complete, and I really need them to go well; so, I try to keep a close eye on them whenever I can sneak a quick second or two. The ladies exit the shower together. I was so focused on work, that apparently, I missed the entire shower scene. 'Not sure which is more disturbing: working on vacation or missing that kind of entertainment.' I get dressed and we exit the room and start our tour of the ship again. By now there are plenty of people on board and the ship is starting to come alive. We step off of the elevator and we commence to people watching; as everyone start to move throughout the vessel.

It's Mona's first time on a cruise ship, so she is decidedly excited about the lights, people, scenery, plants, ambiance, stores and everything else that the ship has to offer. We journey to another; very classy, VIP lounge; that towers over all of the excitement, and provides a three-hundred and sixty-degree angle of the action. We can still people watch while we have cocktails and watch the ship come alive, with new eyes. We find seating that has great views of the action, right at the heart of the ship. "Is there a separate wing, where all of the kids are hiding?" Mona asks, as she snuggles along side of me. Kat and I chuckle; harmoniously. "No – they're not hiding: this is an adult only cruise." Kat explains. I follow with: 'We have the whole ship to ourselves. Trust me when I say that it's more enjoyable this way.' I conclude.

Our waitress arrives: "Hello everyone! My name is Kami, and I'll be your personal host for the evening. Can I start out by getting you any drinks or appetizers?" Kami says as she looks at me, to place my order first. I took the liberty of ordering, given that I love the excitement and happiness that covers their faces, when their taste buds enjoy orgasmic sensations. 'Two Vodka Cranberries and a Classic Mojito with extra lime please' I confirm. "Okay…a gentleman, and he's smart too." Kami says with a bit of sass and flirt in her voice. "Can I get you ladies anything to eat?" she asks. "I was thinking that you would do just fine." Kat mumbles under her breath, to herself; as she sips on her drink. "What was that Hun?" – Kami asks Kat. I snicker which causes me to smile very widely. 'We'll take an order of your: shrimp pot stickers, along with an order of crab and shrimp Bruschetta, and a side of grilled pineapple please.' I include. "Classy, smart, and a Gentleman; who has good taste. Which of you is the lucky girl?" Kami asks. Kat and Mona turn to look at Kami: "I am." both Kat and Mona respond at the same time – while giggling in synchronization. I think that they enjoy creating a certain amount of dubiety: whenever possible.

This clearly confused Kami. She shakes her head a bit, like she's just seen a ghost from her past; that she's trying to convince herself, that she didn't see. 'This is my wife: Kat.' I say, introducing the ladies in efforts to clear confusion. Kat follows with: "and this is our girlfriend Mona. So technically, we both are very lucky as you can see." Kat explains. "Ahh… I see. Looks like you two aren't the only ones that are lucky." – Kami says; as she winks at me and walks away to get our drinks. I smile and she leaves to go get our drinks and food. I turn to Mona just in time, to catch her watching Kami; as she walked away. Apparently, Mona wasn't the only one either. "She has a nice ass and she's cute too." Kat says, in a desirable tone. "I would have to agree with you there." Mona replied. "The things that we could do with her." Mona says, just before smiling and winking at me. "I'm sure someone would love that show." – Mona comments.

Kami arrives back with our drinks, and sits them down individually. "I'll be back shortly with the appetizers." – Kami explains. "Is there anything else that I can do for you in the interim?" she asks, before walking away. "Not right now; however, I would love for you to come and check on us; say later this evening." Kat replies. Kami looks with flattery, and she blushes a bit. "I'm sure that there will be plenty of things that 'you can do for 'us' then." Kat replies. "Anything to accommodate you very special guest and ensure that your stay with us is nothing but pleasure: I mean pleasant of course. What time would you like me?" Kami asks. 'I will send Henry to escort you promptly at ten o'clock p.m.' – I intercede and explain to Kami; before she leaves to collect our food.

'Are my beautiful Queens' having fun yet?' – I ask the Ladies'. Mona seems to be pretty excited about the recent chain of events, and those to follow later this evening too. "I am definitely having the time of my life. I can't believe that I've never been on a cruise before. I'm surely not used to the VIP treatment, so this is flipping amazing!" Mona exclaims with everlasting excitement. "Let's go clean up a bit." Kat says to Mona. The ladies prepare to head to the powder room. I stand in their presence and extend my hand in assistance as they descend down the stairs.

I pull my phone out and check on the market. I try not to work too much when the Queens' are around. I eventually notice a lot of women staring at me and trying to get my attention as they walk past. Seems like an uptick in traffic since the ladies left too. Some gentlemen raise their glasses to me and nod. I nod back raising my glass; giving a classic gentlemen's response. The ladies are on their way back. I stand and offer my hand, once again as they approach. They ascend to their seats with impeccable timing; as Kami approaches with food-in-hand. The ladies place their napkins across their laps. Kat immediately breaks out the chopsticks, and prepare to eat her shrimp dumplings. "Yum…this looks really good." Mona confirms. They both get very excited about food. Both my Queens' are foodies – probably another reason why they get along so well. Together – they will try just about anything. I have more of an exotic meets unique and eclectic, sort of taste.

"How is everything?" Kami asks us; as she approaches. 'It's

very good; thank you.' I reply. "You're welcome, sir." Kami says, in a flirtatiously-subjugated voice, just before walking away. Another platter of food arrives. It's covered; so, I can't immediately tell what it is. 'I'm sorry, but we didn't order that.' – I state. "Compliments of the house, sir." – the waiter expresses; as he extends the plate toward me. I look over toward the bar and there was Kami waiving and winking. She drops her head; as if she were shy. She then raises it slightly; just enough for her eyes to meet mine. She flutters her eyes a couple of times, very slow and seductive like; just before pulling her bottom lip in and biting on it. Kami drops her head, for a final time and walks away. 'Thank you.' – I state to the waiter with a slight bow to the head, giving him the okay to leave the tray.

"Wow Daddy. Looks like you've made a hell of an impression on that young lady." Kat says to me. 'I guess I did; however, I don't think that I did it alone though. I'm quite certain that you two played a role in all of this as well.' – I say, as I look at Kat and Mona with a smile. We order more drinks: the food is phenomenal. I love it when the flavors consort together on my tongue, creating a fuse that's hard to mimic. A different waitress brings the drinks.

'Perhaps Kami is on break or needed elsewhere.' I think to myself. We continue to people watch, drink and eat. There are lots of beautiful women on the ship; that's for sure. The Queens' and I will have a lot of fun on this trication.

We end our short adventure in this lounge; and search for a new one; as we wait for the show that's starting soon, in the Krystal Theatre; where we have balcony seating near the stage. Henry meets us in the lounge and escorts us. 'Ladies first.' I state, as the ladies stand and prepare to advance towards the theater. We arrive swiftly, taking all of the secret passageways; while guided by Henry. They have our drinks already waiting in our designated seats. We sat; as Henry stands next to us, in his Navy-Blue; three-piece-suit, and Camel – Louis Vuitton shoes. The show opens and the stage fills with Burlesque dancers. I glance over at Kat. I love to watch as her face lights up, and she loses herself in the performance. I love the fact that a beautiful woman is capable of allowing her breath to be taken away, by another beautiful woman; without there being a cat fight in the end. She has the most beautiful soul. It's absolutely astonishing; watching such a work of art be both tempted and tame while slowly losing control on the inside. I watch as she timidly starts to cross and uncrosses her legs. Not able to find the position that calms her nerves, so she squirms slightly. I lean over and softly kiss her on her neck allowing my warm breath to precede me; touching her skin before my lips could; causing the hair on her body to stand with excitement. She's already starting to roll her head to the right, leaving her neck open to embrace my kiss; while wanting to run all at the same time. I slowly move up toward her ear, where I gently bite her ear lobe; softly pinching it in between my lips, just before whispering in her ear: "Breathe – Love". She smiles from ear to ear and further composes herself. She turns and kisses me on the lips, and I whisper: 'That's my girl.' I lift her left hand and kiss the back of it; securing my arm around her as we continue to enjoy the show.

There were several scenes that moved Kat hellaciously. She definitely has an appreciation for the arts. The show comes to an end, and we stand and applaud for the performers. "It was a really good show." – Mona stated. "Yes, it was" Kat responds.

Henry escorts us out of our exit, that leads to a private elevator; then back to the suite. Kat drops her clutch onto the table. Mona whimsically falls onto the couch into her favorite spot; as though she was a part of the burlesque show, and it's now continued into our living room. Henry emerges from the Butlers' Pantry with two bottles of wine, glasses, a tray of cheese, and a separate tray with a cigar, cigar-cutter, cedar planks, matches and a crystal ashtray. He set them up on the table and starts to walk toward me. "Sir, I can assume that my services are no longer needed for the remainder of the evening, sir." Henry says – as he glances at Kat and Mona who are currently kissing one another, and making their way upstairs in the process. I pull my money clip from my inside jacket pocket. I take two; one-hundred-dollar-bills, stuff them in Henry's jacket pocket and pat him on the back, while leading him towards the door. 'One last thing.' – I say, before leaning inward toward Henry to speak. I whisper in his ear as he leans in. Afterwards; Henry departs and exits the suite.

I turn and there was Kat upstairs undressing. Mona already completely naked; she reaches in and turns on the shower. Steam slowly fills the glass room. I walk over and pick up my cigar, and I cut the end while watching. I eventually light my cedar plank with a match: like a true gentleman should. I sit back on the couch and watch as Kat finishes undressing. Mona walks over and helps her with the removal of her bra. She runs her hands down Kat's back; following the silhouette of Kat's body with her fingers. Kat is ticklish; so, she flinches and tenses up a bit, but works hard to not let it show. 'What a beautiful creature.' – I think to myself; as Mona's hand sweeps her round plump ass. My Queens' love giving me a show. *"Ding"* – the elevator chimes, and in walks a sylphlike-silhouette; looking like a sexy Dame – as she switches from side-to-side. She walks with confidence, purpose and desire. At glance, she is definitely intriguing, if nothing more. I can hear Kat telling me to: "breathe – Love"; as she stares down at me from above.

Kami walks up to me and takes the cigar from out of my mouth. I smile; as she wraps her sultry, red lips around my cigar and takes a pull. She pulls it out, tongue grazing it; just before she blows the smoke into the air. She sees the Queens', and her jacket constructively falls to the ground; forming a circle around her. She steps out of it and places the cigar back into my mouth. She takes a sip from my cup as she ascends, and heads toward the stairs in her six-inch stiletto's. She removes her bra and leaves it on the bannister at the start of the stairs; slowly clambering towards the

Queens' while undressing at the same time. While in stride, she takes her thongs off, dropping them on the stairs, leaving a trail of pheromones to lead the way. She stops and stares a little dramatic stare as they hit the floor. Completely naked – She captures the attention of Kat and Mona, as she lands at the top.

The Queens' open the door to the shower, and Kami walks in; as she dumps her heels; entering as though she's in a bit of a trance. The Queens' rub all over each-others' bodies; playing, teasing, feeling and soothing one another; as water trickles down, and steam continues to fill the shower. The individual streams of water run across the Queens' nipples, just before following the outline of their bodies; down to the creases of their inner thighs. You can hear the ice in my glass clanking together, as I take the last sip of scotch. I sit my glass down on the table, and take another pull of my cigar. Some of the smoke lingers in my face, before I blow it into the air; while still watching the Queens' play.

I lick my lips, and progress towards the bar to pour another drink from the crystal decanter. I look up at the shower admiring the Queens' as they enjoy one another and keeping each other entertained; until I arrive. The Queens' love using vibrators while in the shower: 'My, my, my... How life has changed.' – I think to myself. I loosen my tie and take another sip of my scotch; while ascending toward the staircase. I grab my cigar and position it, prior to grabbing my glass, and I make my way up.

I slowly start to unbutton my shirt as I walk upstairs. I sit in the chair positioned in front of the glass-enclosed; bathroom, and cross my legs like a gentleman. Kat signals me from the shower – with her seductive eyes and hypnotic gaze. I take another pull from my cigar. Her back pinned against the shower wall, as both Kami and Mona kiss all over her body. I sit and watch; as they enjoy my Queen.

"Daddy..." she whispers to me. The words permeate – like loud white noise in a quiet room; through the steam and across the room – piercing my ears. I smile, and wink at Kat; whispering: 'Bring it to Daddy'; after taking another sip. The Queens' exit the shower following Kat. She leads them to a pink and gray case, where they pause and wait: as instructed. She opens the case and removes two leashes and matching collars; which have the letter "K" engraved on them. Kat smiles and winks at the Queens' as they sit on the bed. She places the collars around their necks. The Queens' are so obedient; that they patiently wait as Kat connects the leashes to their collars. Once attached; she grabs ahold of their collars, and motions the Queens' to the floor.

Kat starts to walk towards me with Mona and Kami crawling on all fours next to her. She hypnotizes me with this seductive walk of hers. I can't help but allow myself to be lost in the moment. Mona and Kami continue to crawl in sync with one another – never moving faster than Kat.

Upon arrival, Mona goes left, while Kami crawls straight to me; positioning her body in between my legs. She spreads my legs – seemingly excited; much like finding her prize at the bottom of her Cracker Jack Box. She slowly and dauntlessly rubs across my chest, making circles with the tip of her finger. She started unfastening the remainder of the buttons on my shirt, and fanned it open. Mona – now behind me; starts kissing on my chest as Kami removes my pants. I look up at Kat who's smoking on my cigar with one hand and holding my drink in the other: "I love you" – She whispers to me, while she stares and look; as the Queens' ravish my body, biting and scratching with anticipation and excitement. Kat puts the glass down, and rest the cigar in the ashtray. She walks over towards me and starts to rub on my head.

She circles me, observing as the ladies enjoy every inch of my body; with her hand never leaving my head. She stops in front of me and raises her leg, placing it on the opposite side of the chair; leaving me direct VIP access. She likes to be teased, so I start kissing on her inner-knee, seductively and passionately; making her squirm. I work my way up her thigh biting and kissing along the way; making her body react to each sensual connection. I look up and watch her as she closes her eyes, to take in each and every single kiss and touch, as though she never wanted them to end. I reach the crease of her thigh and start to tickle it with my tongue.

She rubs my head; as she leans back – pushing my head deeper into her crevice. Pussy so wet, that her kream is running down the side of my lips. The stickiness draws me in closer like a magnet. I bury my face, like an ostrich in the desert. She gets excited and escorts my head to her VIP room: using both hands. Kat moans, drawing the attention of Mona and Kami, who are both vigorously at work themselves; making me wail and quiver. The vibrations forces Kat's warm kream to cover my tongue like whipped-cream; straight from the can. The moaning further arouses Mona and Kami. Mona circles around to Kat, and fervently starts to suck on one nipple; while pinching the other. I change rhythms and focus on her Pussy, while Mona sucks on her nipples. Mona teases Kat, and cuts it short leaving her nerves on edge. With Kat more aroused; her kream starts to flow like lava. Her volcano exploded, drawing the Queens' closer like moths to a flame, as they lick and suck on her legs. The Queens bury their heads' in her pussy, making her legs quiver and shake with euphoria and excitement.

The Queens' then start to rub their sticky lips on my chest; slowly making their way back down to my dick. Kat takes a moment to enjoy the sensations of her orgasm before joining in. All three ladies migrate south. Kami and Mona both stop and take turns embracing my dick; as Kat kneels before me caressing my balls, just before she sucks them into her mouth like a vortex; commanding her warm tongue to softly massages them. The rocking motion of her tongue feeling like a gentle oceans wave, making my nerves grow weak and somewhat unresponsive. As the pleasure intensifies, I grab the arms of the chair and push off; hearing the cracking of the wood underneath the intensity of great head. She uses her tongue as a paintbrush: gently stroking my canvas. The magnificent feeling so unbearable; that I simply have to give into the moment and take it all in. The release was magically pleasurable.

DELIVERANCE

The horn blows loudly, waking me up. The Queens' squirm a bit, but remain unfazed by the noise. The Captain is coming over the intercom and explaining the days travel itinerary, weather, location etc. I keep the intercom on in the suite: simply because I like to be informed. The Queens' are asleep. Their beautiful bodies rest; while draped in soft bamboo sheets. I crawl from in between the Queens, and head downstairs; where breakfast and Henry awaits.

"Good morning, sir. Welcome to the beautiful island of St. Kitts!" Henry says. "Morning Henry." – I reply; as I step out onto the balcony to see the beautiful turquoise blue waters. I take it all in for a moment, giving me a chance to visualize the day planned ahead; which starts off with a nice swim in the ocean, followed with jets skis. I have a special consultant coming out with us for the day.

I'm deep in thought when I hear Henry say: "Sorry to disturb sir, but would you like for me to bring breakfast out on the balcony?" he asks. 'Henry, I think I'll take you up on that offer.' I respond. "Of course-sir; right away." He states. Henry brings out a salmon omelet, with: feta, mushroom, tomato and Serrano peppers; and a side of wheat toast, accompanied by a Strawberry-Lemonade Mimosa. "Everything is ready to go, as you requested." – Henry states.

Henry motions to hand me a silver tray with Kat's food on it. I had her favorite breakfast prepared: "A veggie omelet with a half a bagel, (the top half only) and a small bowl of gravy, complimented by a glass of strawberry mimosa, and a red rose – in a small thin vase for madam." Henry recites as he sits down. He has an identical tray in his hands with Mona's favorite on it: "Quiche and a small bowl of shrimp with grits and a half-sliced banana covered in chocolate, complimented by a watermelon lemonade mimosa, with a pink rose in a small identical vase." - he concludes.

I walk into the room while Henry waits outside the door. The ladies still asleep, as I come around to the left side of the bed, and bend down to give Kat a soft kiss. She immediately began to stretch; making the cutest face while doing so. 'Good morning, Love.' – I say as, she looks up at me smiling. "Good morning.": she responds. "Beautiful as always." – I tell her. "Who me? Stop it!" – Kat says in a bashful way. "I just woke up." she says. "Yes, you did Love, and you are as beautiful; as always." – I say, as I kiss her on her forehead. Kat smiles a huge smile and laughs. "You are so silly." – she exclaims gently.

I extended the arms on her tray and placed it over her legs; just before removing the decorative silver dome plate cover. "Thank you, Daddy." – Kat says. She makes me smile as usual. 'You are welcome, Love.' I say, as I turn and walk out; to get the next tray from Henry. I walk to the opposite side of the bed and give Mona a soft kiss, good-morning. "Good Morning Poppi." she says as she sits up with a sweet smile and leans over to give Kat a kiss. I placed the tray over her lap. "Enjoy breakfast in bed my darlings." "Daddy, where are you going?" Kat asked. I look back: 'I'm gonna eat breakfast on the balcony – My Love.' I say with a smile, as I look back and respond. 'She has the sexiest sleepy face.' – I think, as I make my way out the door.

Once on the balcony, I pull their chairs out for them; before taking a seat to eat. If I know my Queens'; they'll be here soon. I take a call… Shortly after, some figures fade from the background and the door swings open. Its Henry, followed by two beauties wearing sheer robes, with nothing but thongs and a bra underneath… I put my call on hold, and I stand to greet them: "I knew you two would not stay in bed." I say, as they each kiss me – prior to me pushing their chairs in.

Henry exits the suite carrying their breakfast trays. I step away to finish my call, as they indulge in their food. I return to the table: "Was that Felix?" Kat asks me. 'Yes.' – I answer, as I look at Kat with slow anticipation, given her current and familiar tone of voice. 'How'd you know?' – I asked. "I think that you should cancel the deal." Kat says, with a straight face. I look at Kat and ask: 'Why is that, My Love?' "Not sure yet, it just came to me in a dream" Kat says. "There were buildings falling down everywhere." 'This is a billion-dollar deal, Love.' - I stated in a calm voice. "I'm aware, Daddy…" – Kat says to me, right before she looks at me with those eyes. "Walk away…" Kat says with credence. I pick up my phone: 'Lilly, cancel the waterfront- resort deal with Felix. Just cancel it, and please send me those leads that we tucked away.' - I conclude, upon ending the call. 'Done.' – I say, as I kiss Kat on the forehead. 'You ladies ready for what Daddy has planned for you today?' I ask. I sure am Poppi." Mona replies with exhilaration. "What are we doing?" she asks, in a very alluring and seductive manner while continuously arching her eyebrows, in excitement. I look at Mona and smile. 'Henry, can you please bring the ladies their itineraries for the day?' I ask. Henry brings over some very fancy stationery for the ladies. They each open their individual envelope, and read their itineraries; as huge smiles stretch across their faces. "Daddy – these activities require that your hair gets wet…" Kat says as she looks at me with confusion.

"Where my Queens' at?" – Darian screams at the top of his lungs; as Henry holds the door open. Kat's eyes light up, and she stands up to go greet him. "What are you doing here?" – Kat asks. "Gurl… you know I couldn't have you out here looking crazy. When Mr. Man sent me my ticket, I packed my bags, and… Boom girl, my ass is here… Now tell me what the hell we getting into today?" – Darian concludes. At that moment, Henry walks over and hands Darian his itinerary. "Oh shit. It's laminated and everything. Somebody means serious business." he yells. Darian opens the itinerary like it was a Christmas Present; damn near tearing it to shreds. "Gurl… I can't wait: matter-of-fact, where's the bathroom at? We need to get this process started right now…" Kat just giggles, with the most simplistic smile gracing her face. "Mona Love – how are you Darlin?" Darian ask as he hugs her really tight; while they do a little shake and dance. "You Queens' ready for all of this?" Darian screams with surprise and joy. "I'm so excited"; he states, as he shimmies into the suite. Kat enters behind Darian; as they head to the bathroom and prepare to start the "process": as Darian calls it.

Mona reaches for my glass and quickly finishes it, before leaving me to join them. I stand to greet her: like a gentleman should. With a surprise attack, she grabs me by the neck with her left hand; as she licks me from the back of my neck-to the tip of my lips; while holding my balls with her right hand. She groans: "bye Poppi". I smile and bite the bottom of my lip. 'I really just want to fuck the shit out you right now.' I say to Mona as smiles with anticipation. "I know…" – she whispers in my ear, just before departing; leaving me frozen in time; with my heart beating rapidly. Henry places another drink in front of me almost instantaneously; as laughter pervades in the background. 'Thank you, Henry: right on time as usual.' I say. "Thank you, Sir," Henry says. "Is there anything else I can get you, sir?" he asks. 'No, not right now:

Henry.'

Mona runs towards the bathroom where Darian and Kat are. "So glad that you could come." – Kat says to Darian as, she darts towards him for another hug. "Girl, I'm just glad that I got the ticket. You know that I love me some – 'Mr. Man', nawh…" he says in his Southern, Big-Mommies-voice; concluding with: "And you too, of course." Kat just smiles from ear to ear. "Of course." she responds. "Speaking of you and Mr. Man. How are things with Miss Mona?" – Darian asks, with emphasis. "Things with Mona are really good. She's: bright, funny, sexy, gorgeous, respectful, open, transparent and submissive… She's: self-sufficient, enticing, helpful, goofy as hell, yet sophisticated and she understands her place. She's: confident and a force to be reckoned with at times. She's perfect… She understands and knows who she is, and she understands, and owns her role in this bond and we all wake up happy each morning." Kat concludes, with a smile. Darian's starring at Kat with that signature look that says: "I still think that your crazy as hell: and full of shit too." Kat smiles her signature smile; in response.

"We adore her." – Kat assures him; as she glows with pure excitement. "You adore me too; got room for one more?" –

He asks; with sarcasm and a snickering laugh. Both Kat and Darian laugh out loud. "I wanna laugh too…" – Mona says as she enters the room. "Girl get over here; so, we can get this *hair* did." Darian says to Mona, with that southern-twang, again. "What'd you comb this hair with this morning: a brush made of wool?" Darian asks, in his snarky, yet funny yet, loving. "Well if you must know; I had a long night…" – Mona responds as she swings her hair, whipping Darian's face, in the process.

They have their fun, and after hours of covering the entire bathroom in accessories that I can't identify, they emerge: photo shoot ready. 'Gorgeous as ever My Loves.': I compliment. "Thank you, Daddy!" the Queens' say in harmony. "Darian, you look stunning as ever, too." I say – considering that he was rocking his entire body back and forth – opposite his eyes; much like that cat-clock that hangs on your grand-mothers' kitchen wall. "Thank You – Daddy." Darian says in an impish and sarcastic tone, as he walks behind the ladies, while smiling and giggling. I just smirk, shake my head and laugh.

I proceed to follow as; Henry leads the group once again.

We enter the elevator and proceed to our private exit – where our car awaits. Darian enters the car first. Kat looks at her watch and says: "Oh no, were going to be late." Exclaiming with excitement. I swing down to her beautiful lips, and kiss her gently. 'Already taken care of love.' I state, as she smiles with that look that says: "You make my heart flutter." I smile back with a look that says: "You've always made my heart flutter – Love." I wait for her to enter the vehicle; Mona enters next and kisses me on the lips as well. I smile because I know that she is being silly, and I absolutely love it. Kat turns on some music, and they immediately begin to chime-in; singing along with the song. Eventually, all three start to sing in harmony.

Mona hands me a bottle. I pull the foil back and pop the cork. I pour a few glasses of champagne and the partying began. I look around the car, and smile; as I watch everyone enjoy themselves and have a good time. The energy was more than vitalizing. 'A bit under developed, in a great location, vibrant and a great opportunity to invest in.' – I quickly think to myself. I pull out my phone and proceed to send an email, until a soft touch quickly averts my attention elsewhere. "You're supposed to be relaxing…" Kat says with the softest voice. 'I am Love. I just see great opportunity here and I need to get the ball rolling before someone else does.' She gives me a look of concern, assuming that I am one email away from making this a: work deal vs. a vacation. She rubs my hand with her right hand; to ensure that I can feel her touch. An instant calm comes over me and she whispers: "Breathe – My Love: Trust me.". We stare at each other as though it was our first-time meeting. We break the silence with a smile, and we each take a sip from our glass; as the sun reflects beautifully off of her skin flickering back and forth. The car stops; breaking the spell-like gaze. We arrive at our destination, and you hear Henry's door slams shut. My door opens and I exit the car, Mona exits next, and Kat thereafter – with Darian following.

We enter this exotic private beach club where the ambiance is created with sophistication, excellence and luxury in mind while; accommodating a lifestyle of elegance, and self-fulfillment. It sets the mood, preparing our expectations for what's to come. We enter our suite; which has ocean views and a private beach. The suite doors open, and there are three ladies waiting to serve us; each holding a tray of hors d'oeuvres. One of the Queens' is looking at Kat with a plumb motion; as though she was on the menu. Kat loves to flirt; so, she quickly tuned into the advances that this stunning creature was making. Kat touches the right side of the young ladies' face, as they gaze into each other eyes. With her single pointer finger; Kat makes it down to the jaw line, leaving Mona feeling possessive and jealous. Her finger softly falls off of the edge of her face.

Mona happens to be close by and practically catches Kat's finger as it falls – placing it in her mouth. Slowly sucking upwards until it makes a *pop* sound; as Kat's finger exits her grasp. "Just wanted to make sure that your hands were clean before you ate, Love." - Mona says with assertiveness, as she gives off a very passive and sarcastic smile, that says: "She's mine. Back off Bitch." - as she all but growled at the young lady. "Umm…Go-head-on-now: little girl…" Darian says, as he sits his bags down on the table. I shake my head in considerable unsureness.

We get acquainted and settle in. There are all sorts of desserts and hors d'oeuvres in the kitchen, and the bar is fully stocked as well. I take a call as the Queens' go change into their swimsuits. Kat gives me that look as my phone rang. 'I'll be done before you can close the door – Love.' I say. "Promise?" – she asks with a smile; as she gives me a kiss and takes off to get changed. I hang up, telling Lilly that I'm not taking any more calls today.

I walk up to the bar and placed my order, prior to stepping out onto the veranda. The Queens' enter the room. Stunning as always: of course. I expected nothing less. 'I love the way Kat's radiance, precedes her beautiful face.' – I think to myself. We exit onto the veranda and take a seat next to the pool; so that we can people watch. We sit up a little higher, which makes it easier to see all of the people mingling below. "I want to hit the skis' now, as opposed to later." Mona says. "Come on…you know you're dying to play too." she continues; as she's tugging on Kat and I – much like a spoiled child. Kat and Mona stare at one another; just before taking off in full stride toward the water. Darian and I just look at each other, laugh and slightly shake our heads. I admire the ladies as they run off, wearing my two favorite colors: Hunters Green and Passion Red. Their jet skis are ready and waiting. The Queens' hop on their skis, screaming: "come on you two." Darian and I make our way down towards them: we suit up, and the race is on.

We each hit the water: "No teams and may the best rider win." Mona screams; and we're off. Kat's in the lead, and I'm right behind her. Mona soon takes the lead from Kat and Darian follows. He steals first and keeps it. Kat tries to take the lead: passing me. My jet ski seems like it's getting slower and slower. It's slowing down more and more; eventually coming to a halt. My crew is already docked back at the club; before they notice that I'm missing.

"Where's Daddy?" – Kat asks; as she's looking around. She grabs the binoculars: "I don't see his jet ski – oh there he is. He's swimming back." Kat shouts with excitement. "Girl, get the boat, call somebody; don't let that handsome thang get eaten by sharks and drown." Darian screams in hysteria and panic. Mona and Kat are starring at Darian as though he's lost his damn mind. "Stop panicking like a little Bitch." Mona says to Darian. Kat can't help but choke on the saliva that was attempting to go down, when that punch in the throat was delivered; re-routing the saliva on a detour, to an incorrect pipe, that was only meant for wind. She closes her eyes and shakes her head with deep concern for Mona.

Darian has this look that says: "I don't know what to think

about what this Bitch just said to me." He has half of a serious face; but only half, because the other half looks like it's already smiling. They all burst into laughter. I arrive on shore. The Queens' run, grab towels, and attempt to dry me off, as they blot me down. Darian grabs one from their hands and starts to blot me down as well, in a very comical; yet mama-bear – kind of way. Kat and Mona just stare at each other and shake their heads in utter amazement; just before they simultaneously laugh out loud at Darian. I tap both my Queens' three times and we head towards the suite. Kat's eyebrows rise, as she asks Darian: "Everything okay; Darlin? He made it and he's okay, right." Kat asks in a tone that helps him think rationally; while smiling and shaking her head – all the while.

She thinks that it's cute. 'I'm still not one-hundred percent sure as to what I should be thinking; but I'm in good hands so, I'm not too worried.' – I think to myself; as I look back in witness. We go back to the beach club and lay out on the veranda. I wash under the shower really well, prior to laying out on the lounge chairs. Kat brings me a plate of food over. I love it when she pampers me. The plate has smoked oysters, shrimp and lobster claws; accompanied by a side of red wine and a vast array of other complimenting sauces to further enhance the flavor.

The Queens aren't hungry yet, so Kat takes an oyster off of my plate and slurps it down in a way that turns me thee fuck on. She held it up in the air, and seduces it into her mouth; using only her tongue, as a utensil.

'What a wicked beast: that tongue of hers.' - I think to myself. Kat places the oyster shell down on my plate, kisses me with her wet tongue and walks over to join Mona in the pool. I watch for a while as they swim. While submerged underwater, the sunlight makes a shimmery silhouette off of their bodies. I watch every stroke and turn: their silhouettes becoming more addicting – as I follow. I sat gazing, and what were once minutes, quickly turns to hours. Simple happiness, and not a care in the world. The sun glistens off of their bodies, magnifying their already benevolent beauty.

"Sir, I am sorry to disturb – but I need to inform you that the boat is here to take you on to your next adventure, sir." Henry says, as he disrupts my angelic trance. 'Perfect Henry, thank you.' I respond. "Also – sir, I wanted to take the time to introduce: Natalia. She will be my replacement, looking after the Ladies' while were away. She's my equal in that respect, sir." Henry concludes. I crouch down next to the pool – as the Queens' swim up. 'Listen… Looks like my ride is waiting for me, so I gotta go. I'm taking Henry with me, and Natalia here will be taking good care of you both, while were away. There is a nice surprise waiting for you both; in my absence so, enjoy and don't play too hard.' – I advise. They smile as water drips from their foreheads and bead off of their faces. I kiss them both, and proceed to the boat with Henry. We load up and take off as the Queens' wave goodbye.

Once out of their sight; Natalia asks: "Are you ladies ready to start your adventure?" "Yes, ma'am." – Mona answers. Natalia smiles: "Follow me please." she says. The Queens' exit the pool and follow Natalia through the resort, and to the private spa. They enter a private elevator, which opens up to the exclusive spa area, like a penthouse: if you will. The spa is lined with white and black marble. The benches and massage tables were marble, with elegant soft under lighting that illuminated, making the room feel comfortable and soothing. There are masseuses waiting near each table for the Queens. Natalia escorts them to a partition; that will cover them as they undress. Both Kat, and Mona each wrap their towels around their bodies and proceed to the steam room, once finished. They have to lay in there for a while, allowing their pores to open up before they can proceed to the next phase of the process.

The Queens' are then escorted to special tables, just outside the steam room; where they were smothered with a honey and cucumber mix, that's spread onto the skin. Once completed; they phase back to the steam room, where they spend more time – allowing the formula to work its way into the skin, as the pores open. Afterward; Kat and Mona head to the shower and rinse off; allowing the steam and pressure from the jets to do the work for them, and making the experience both fun and exhilarating.

While basking under the pressure of the jets, they've seemingly captured the attention of Natalia. Mona observing her, as she peaks; consistently watching Kat as she washes the sticky honey from her body, leaving Mona to smile. They exit the shower and wrap their towels around them preparing to move over to the massage room. Natalia escorts them into the parlor, where the masseuse directs them to lie on the massage beds, face down; first. They prepared a special blend based off of some of Kat's favorite oils that I shared with them, upon booking the appointment. The masseuses' drizzles the oil over their bodies and softly caresses it in; allowing it to penetrate the skin prior to massaging the unique blend in afterwards. The typical spa-relaxation, music is playing in the background. The smell of lavender and lemon grass – mixed with a hint of eucalyptus oil is permeating throughout the room, helping to calm; as the massaging of the body does the rest.

Natalia tries to hide the fact that she's attracted to the two of them, by glancing out of her peripheral, as the Queens bodies are being touched and worked by the masseuse; as they lay across the warm slabs.

With the massage coming to an end, the Queens' are once again, escorted to the steam room where they are covered in more honey and oils; prior to being wrapped in seaweed – this time. After sitting in there for five minutes, they are moved to the mud-room, where they slowly make entry to the cold-pool of mud. The Queens' huddle together to create body heat. They slowly start to rub their own arms, with one hand crossed over the other; covering their chests. Mona walks over to Kat and immediately starts to rub her arms for her; as she shivers.

In an attempt to increase body heat, the Queens' start to rub on each-other's arms, swiftly stroking up and down in a repetitive motion, thinking that this would be a better alternative. Softly stroking and rubbing in every nerve-bearing, square-inch, crack, crevice and curve; Mona slowly moves up to Kat's perky nipples, and starts to softly flick them with the tip of her thumb. Kat closes her eyes and lives in the moment with arousal and satisfaction – as her guided focus. So aroused, they prematurely exit the mud bath; back into the shower. The temp quickly changes from cool to warm; upon entrance, leaving Kat's nipples hard again. Mona covers the entire areola with her mouth, taking the temp from cool to warm, while making Kat squirm.

Natalia is locked in a trance right now – hypnotized by the synchronization of their bodies: she can't stop looking and watching. They have her full attention and these Queens' can't help but put on a show. They exit the shower and make their way into the dessert room; holding hands, flirting and teasing the entire way there. There are two concierges waiting outside of the room, with desserts on a tray: one on each side of the door. Chocolate covered cherries, strawberries and brownie bites are offered amongst other erotic delights.

Kat grabs a chocolate covered strawberry and takes a bite out of it, while Mona picks up a chocolate covered cherry and locks it gently in with her beautiful, pearly-white, teeth. She uses her skills to seduce the concierge with the stem. Swirling it around on her bright pink tongue; Mona turns and extends the cherry out of her mouth as though she was making an offering to Kat. Still chewing on what remained of her chocolate covered strawberry; Kat smiles as she watches Mona seductive attempts at foreplay. Enticed and turned on even more so, she walks over to Mona and removes the cherry from her tongue – with only her lips to assist. Mona moans, and kisses Kat on the lips as she chews on her cherry. Her moans immediately infuse Kat's nerves; flooding her vagina walls.

She smiles and Mona notices that there is a small speck of

chocolate on the crevice of Kat's mouth. Mona smiles back in a seductive and attractive way; as she moves in to lick the speck off, using only the tip of her pointy tongue. Bothered and ready to join in on the fun, Natalia opens the door for the Queens' to enter and play with privacy. She's starring with anticipation, as though she was waiting for an invite; meanwhile the Queens' were busy licking and sucking the chocolate off of each other's faces. Kat opens her eyes to see Natalia starring and biting on her bottom lip. Kat smiles and stops kissing Mona; leaving her frozen in a moment that she was not prepared to end.

She walks to the bed, and picks through the chocolate selection; biting on some, while leaving others. Kat slowly walks towards the door; seducing Natalia with her eyes the entire time. One hand on the door; Natalia's eyes can't stop gazing into Kat's. It's both a gift and a curse. She can seduce you without saying a word. Her eyes talk to you, and summon you to her, much like the voice of a siren. She'll seduce you, even when she's not trying to. She slowly pushes the door close with her left hand; while biting on her right index finger, as though there was residual chocolate or Mona on it. She walks towards Mona with a seductive sway, and they continue to engage in their erotic and orgasmic fun.

They roll around on the bed, which is covered in chocolate, and whipped cream, while getting messy and playing with their food: which is Kat's favorite thing to do. They are very messy and cloaked in chocolates, and all sorts of other colorful fruit too. They lick each other all over; leaving tongue marks through what was once caked on chocolate.

"*Beep, beep,*" the horn signal as the boat approaches. The deck hand tosses the line onto the dock to another worker. I can see the frustration on Henry face. He's not pleased; not pleased at all. 'That's funny. I should be the one who's upset.' – I think to myself. I step onto the dock and instantly, I feel the boat push away from beneath me. I hear Henry: "Sir. Once again, I do apologize…" He states. 'Henry' – I say, as I place my hands on his right shoulders; trying to insure him that everything things is fine. 'It's ok. Really, these things are uncontrollable, and it's not your fault; or anyone's fault – for that matter.' I say while speaking loud enough for the captain to hear too. She hasn't said a word in hours. The look of shame, and embarrassment all rolled up in one is displayed across her face. Darian steps off the boat, rolls his eyes as hard as he could and stormed off saying: "This has been one hell of an outing." he exclaims. 'That's a lot of drama in one package.' – I say; as Darian stomps away.

We follow Darian; making our way back up the dock, toward the clubhouse. The Queens' exit onto the veranda with chocolate caked into their hair; leaving a trail of dessert as it drops from their bodies. They're giggling, and of course – I think it's adorable; however, Darian – not so much. He looks at them too, and rolls his eyes even harder than before, and I just didn't think that, that was possible. He enters the suite and slams the door behind him; clearly making a statement, allowing his actions to speak vs. his words.

After having a front row tickets to the show; Kat stares at me in confusion; while trying to not let that moment spoil her fun. I shake my head signaling that there's nothing to worry about.

SYNERGY

Crackling thunder and heavy rain pretty much has everyone indoors for the day; not discounting the incredibly, insane-souls; that thought it was a good idea to sit poolside, in this type of weather. We sit on the covered balcony watching the storm. The storm disrupts the ocean water; which causes the boat to rock more, now so, than before. The stabilizers are set, but the storm is so heavy; that the ride is still very choppy. The captain comes over the intercom advising that: "everything is okay, and that we would be experiencing these choppy waters, for the next several hours, and advises that we've slowed down to four knots, because of it."

In the meantime; Mona falls ill: 'The choppy ride combined with her vertigo must have has gotten the best of her.' I think to myself. I glance over at the Queens'; as Mona lay across Kat's lap on the couch. Kat strokes her head in a consistent and soothing pattern, as she watches television. She's using the television as a distraction for Mona; while she hits some major pressure points that will subdue her vertigo and put her back into balance. The television will take her mind off of things, keeping her muscles focused, and relaxed; while ensuring that Kat's efforts aren't for nothing. Henry enters the suite with the specific ingredients that I've asked for. The Queens' enjoy my special soup when they are sick. Henry sits the groceries down on the counter: 'Thank you, Henry.' I state. "My pleasure sir." – Henry says as he walks away. I get up and start to prepare the meal. I turn the TV off, and the music on. The soft mellow tones flow through the room, as the storm cuts up outside. It takes me roughly thirty to forty-five minutes to finish the entire creation. I carry the food in on a tray; over to the Queens'. Mona sits up with Kat's assistance, and I place the tray on the table, directly in front of them. Kat feed's Mona as though she was a, wee little baby. The Queens' finish and Henry comes to help me with the trays.

We chill and watch TV for the remainder of the day. I find the *OWN* network, and we watch it on a continuous loop, hour-after-hour. I used to set the station to *Lifetime,* when Kat would get sick; but I guess lots has changed now. I fall asleep in between the Queens', while they continue to watch. As long as they are content: I'm happy too. They poke me as I fall asleep, in an attempt to gain my attention. I eventually fall asleep without tiny fingers in my side. Loud thunder cracked; sounding as though it hit the boat. I awake;

as Mona jumps in fear of the loud noise. The lights flicker just before the entire cabin goes dark and Mona covers me like a thin layer of skin. Concerned with all that this could mean; I call out, for a status report: 'Henry.' I shout. "I'm already on it sir. The captain has me on hold for now." Henry responds, just as a big wave crashes against the boat. The lights are still out, which actually starts to frighten the Queens' a bit. I try to take their minds off of things – so I lay back down, trusting that Henry is on top of everything. This calms the Queens' a bit more too. 'Do you Queens' remember the first day we met?' – I ask in an attempt to focus their minds elsewhere. "YES!" – Mona screams as the lights turn back on.

We all exit the room as though we needed air to breathe. I go out onto the balcony to see what all of the ruckus is about. I stay out there for a bit and enjoy watching the thunder as it ripples through the sky; lighting it up like nothing, that I've ever seen before. I find peace and solace under the chaos and friction. I feel whole and at peace. There's a certain kind of calm that lives in the night. It calls me like a moth to a flame: Kat understands that better than anyone. She's watched me sit out in a storm for hours and hours; enjoying the rainfall. I can recall a few times where she's had to remind me to come inside; in some pretty unsafe conditions, that grew so rapidly; that I didn't even notice. The lights go out again; however, Henry is already prepared with his candles, and already started lighting them all around the suite. 'Would you like some help, Henry' I ask. "No sir, I'm fine; Thank you." Henry responds.

I go over to the bar and pour me a drink, as Henry continues to light the candles around the suite. I join the Queens' on the couch. "It's pretty cozy in here." Mona says. while her sweater hangs off her one shoulder; as she lays back onto the couch in a resting position. The lights flicker as Kat slowly pulls her silk blanket over her feet, and up her thighs. Her hips were fully engulfed by the soft, delicate fabric. I watch as her skin slowly forms goose bumps; that covers her entire body. Appearing like little stars on a map, I follow them blindly; wondering what mystical treasures – lie ahead. I continue to watch intensely as her nips starts to form beneath her shirt, causing it to rise – just a hair.

I work to resist the urge to pick her up and take her into the room, close the door behind us, and have my way with her.

Placing her down gently onto the bed, I use my hand to brace the side of her thighs for extra security. I forcefully pull her body in close to mine. She let out a loud gasp, followed by a soft moan; as she quickly wraps her legs around my body, while locking her ankles in the process. I surmise that she was trying to keep me in one spot... Unfortunately, that wasn't going to be the case this time. Kat always said that: "storms bring out my primal side". I plant my hips, and lift her up. She's locked her fingers behind my head, and shifted her weight down; swallowing me whole. The warm sensation feels amazing, heavenly and simple: A nice, tight, fit all the way to the sweet end. Her hair begins to bounce up and down, in a rhythmic motion, as did her voluptuous breast – so perky and tenderly-perfect; in every way. Her warm, sweet, sticky, nectar races down my legs, quickly and quietly, like lava flowing from a volcano. Our synergy is eternal, and connections heighten; as our souls grew closer, and closer under the energy and power of the thunder and lightning.

The storm grew more intense; thunder crashing down like balls of uncontrolled and chaotic energy surrounding us. She erupts, releasing all over me; while biting my neck as though she had no other choice. I give her one last thrust; allowing my baby everything her heart desires, and in this moment: nothing else matters... Just me, her and simply orgasmic pleasure.

I held Kat in my arms. Her head resting on my shoulders, as she carefully pulls her nails from deep within my skin; one-by-one. Her French manicure now stained with blood. 'All is fair.': I think to myself. "Daddy!" She moans in concern; as she actually realizes what's happened – stating: "Let me clean this, so it doesn't get infected." in her motherly-concerned voice. She placed her herbs and oils from inside the nightstand; up-top. "Oh yeah; I'm always ready." Kat says, as she snickers, while setting up shop. Mona appears – standing at the door; revealed as Kat walks off, toward the bathroom. She looks at me with those eyes. 'I know that she was watching.': I think to myself.

Kat returns with a cool towel, and wipes my wounds. Lightning strikes, and a bludgeon force of thunder followed. Startled by the unidentified noise; Kat jumped, making me grab her at the waist. I glance upward and there she was; watching again. My hands simultaneously brace Kat's body, which causes her to moan with both excitement, and pleasure. Her body rolls backwards and she arches her back; as she gets lost in the moment. She loves so differently. 'What an interesting creature: she is.' – I say to myself. 'I'm so glad that she's all mine.' – I think quietly; as I start to kiss on her chest, and prepare to hold her in my arms for the remainder of the night.

BONDS

'Henry' – I call out. "Yes sir, is there something I can do for you?" – he answers. 'Can you grab me a case of wine and four cigars please, and bring them out onto the deck?' – I ask. "Of course; sir, right away, sir." Apparently, I walked out just in time to be greeted by a gush of wind that was waiting, just so it could slap me in the face. The cool air is very refreshing. I can sit here all-day, long. I close my eyes and meditate. Once I'm deep in thought; it's like an endless game, of tug-of-war, to get me out.

Henry returns with the items that I requested. He placed the crate on the counter, in the bar area. I snatch three bottles, and pop the corks; then place two cigars in my shirt pocket. I walked up stairs to the master suite, where the Queens' are stretched across the bed. "Well I'm not sure what they are talking about": Is what I hear as I enter the room. Instantly, Darian sits up with extreme excitement; as if I were Santa Clause on Christmas Eve. "Let's party bitches."– he screams; as he grabs a bottle and takes it to the head.

Mona jumps up, bouncy and smiling as she crawls to me, gazing a seductive look into my eyes; communicating in a language that only her and I currently understand. "Thank you, Poppi." - she says, as she kisses me and takes the bottle from my hand. 'You are so welcome.' – I say. I pull out two cigars for the Queens'. I was able to find Kat's; favorite flavor. Mona is more of a novice when it comes to cigars. "Care to join us?" Kat asks. 'Soon Love. I'm going back onto the balcony for a while.' – I respond. "Not for too long: I hope." She replies 'Of course not, Love. I would never keep you waiting.' I respond. I can feel her stares, so I glance over at Mona, as she gives me that look. The one that lets you know that she is willing to fulfill your every desire.

I give the Queens' a kiss before exiting the room. This storm won't let us be, and I want to get some meditation in before we're locked inside again. I sit there for a while listening to the thunder. A tap on the shoulder takes me out of my state of mind. "I'm sorry to disturb you sir, but I was wondering if I could have a moment of your time."; Henry says. I could instantly tell by the look on his face that this conversation was going to be a serious one. 'Of course, have a seat; but before we get started give me one minute.' – I say, as I walk away. "No worries, Sir; take your time." Henry responds. This conversation seems like it's going to need a little something extra; as Henry never approaches me with such tone and gesture.

I pull out a few bottles of wine from the fridge, and bring the bottles onto the balcony. I place one in front of Henry and sit down with the other placed in front of me. He begins to express what's been weighing on his shoulders. He goes on to tell me about his husband, who has been asking Henry to have a threesome for the longest of time. As I listen more and more, it seems as if Henry is bi-sexual, but his husband is not; which can cause a little conflict. Henry is definitely feeling insecure and not sure how to approach the situation.

I pour Henry a drink. "Oh no Sir… I couldn't, I still have work to do!" Henry exclaims. I look off into the distance for a bit and ponder on the statement. 'You know what… you're right. Henry: You have the rest of the night off. Now that you are off for the night, are you really going to let me waste an entire bottle of vintage wine; Henry?' I say with a bit of sarcasm. He shook his head and smiled. 'What can I do for you; Henry?'. He picked up the bottle of wine and quickly looked for a glass. I intercept and grab the bottle instead stating: 'Not tonight – My Friend. I can tell something is troubling you; so, were taking it straight from the bottle; so, loosen the jacket, the tie and get comfortable." – I say. He places his jacket on the arm of the chair, loosens his tie and takes the bottle straight to the head. "Can I speak freely, Sir?" he asks. 'Absolutely Henry. What's on your mind?' I respond. "How do you do it, sir?" Henry asks. 'How do I do what, Henry?' – I respond. "How can you love two women, at the same time?" I smile and grin with a little chuckle to follow.

The smile on my face may have confused him. He continues with: "I only ask because, my husband wants us to have a threesome; he claims that it would be good for both of us. I won't lie, sir. At first, I thought he was full of himself, and it left me with lots of thoughts and questions; but after having you all as guest, and seeing how you interact with one another: I'm even further confused, and I'm having second thoughts: yet again." Henry concludes.

"I'll admit that when I looked at a relationship such as yours…in the past – I would have prejudged you all. I would have assumed that 'this guy'; is just like any other 'player'; in that you were able to find two insecure women; but that's not always the case; is it sir?" he asks. 'No sir, it is not…' – I respond. 'It's actually more of a reflection of the human-being doing the judging; Henry. It's also typically the root of that person's problem; in relation to the respective subject. Henry, let me ask you a question or two. Do you love him?' – I ask. "Of course, sir." Henry responds. 'Most often, the answers are so simple, that we all miss them.' – I state. "I want you to consider a few things. What would you gain if you were to move forward? Next: consider what you would lose.

Now consider what you would lose if you didn't move forward... Is your gain bigger than your loss?' – I ask with suspense and a perplexed look on my face. 'Here lies the real question Henry: If not: Why not?' 'See – if you stay true to your feelings and emotions that define you; you'll be able to answer those questions with honesty and gain clarity; through contrast. It heals as much as it hurts; but it's a good kind of hurt.' – I explain, as I chuckle, remembering the words of Kat; that helped me to define this moment.

Henry leans back in his chair and thinks long and hard. "I guess when either of us are out of town for a long stint, it would be nice to have someone around to keep the other of us company." – Henry states. I smile at Henry's response. 'Give those some thought; Henry, and let's revisit when you are ready.' I reply. 'Cheers.' – I say as we lift our bottles to toast. "To life." – Henry replies; just before turning up. "One question for you sir." – Henry states: "If God were sitting next to you, would you do anything differently, sir?"

'Henry, the Divine Spirit sits with me every day, and every day, we work together to teach me to be a better man. So, I guess my answer would be, 'no': I wouldn't change a thing.'

ELATIONS

Mona eyes rolled to the back of her head, a clear sign assuring me that I've pinpointed the right spot. Her knees begin to buckle, so Kat slowly positioned Mona across the arms of the chair: on all fours with knees and hands side-by-side – Kat stood in front of Mona pushing her head down slightly, causing the elevation of her ass; bringing it closer to eye view. She puts her foot on the arm of the chair, next to Mona. I lick my fingers and slide right into Kat. This position leaves me to please both Queens' at once.

My body begins to twitch. So, aroused and caught up in the moment; I almost forgot about Kami. I look down, and see Kami still enjoying herself, and loving every minute. I smile, as I look into her pretty eyes: 'Good girl' – I whisper; as she gazes up with her lips perfectly wrapped around my dick. She starts to suck harder; knowing that she's going to make me kum in her mouth. It's as if she's daring and tempting me; almost luring me.

I focus. Both Queens' begin to moan heavily and erupt almost simultaneously; with Kat leading the way. She squirts all over Kami, causing Mona to do the same. Kami looks up with the biggest smile on her face. She consistently surprises me, and she's no stranger to giving great head: that's for sure. Kami slurps all over me; as though she enjoyed every drop. The Queens' rub the love all over Kami's body. She becomes more aroused with each stroke. Her glazed nipples back at attention. Kat smiles and squeezes them harder and harder; as Kami's moans flare.

Mona sticks her fingers inside, causing Kami to really moan and squirm with anticipation, and thrill; her body, begging for more arousal and satisfaction. Kami starts to suck even harder. 'I see that someone's fired up and motivated.' – I think to myself. She pulls herself in closer, bringing me deeper into her throat. She gags on my kum… and I fucking love it. 'Good girl' – I say to her. Her tactics send off a sudden vibration that I can feel; as my head descends further down into her throat; driving me absolutely insane. "Oh, my goodness." Kami yelps, as she starts to flow freely; shooting across the room.

All of the excitement starts to overwhelm me. I erupt in Monas mouth – coating the inside of those sexy cheeks, as the feelings intensifies. It rushes to the back of her throat, sliding down to the pit of her stomach; as she swallows. The slurping sound drives me mad, and does something to my nerves. 'That's it baby…Don't stop.' I groan. With so much to give, Mona had no choice but to retreat momentarily; allowing herself opportunity to breathe. She unsuccessfully does her best not to spill anything. No worries though; she quickly slurps it back up, and swallows it all; once she reforms. Mona sees Kami's face dripping wet, and starts licking the excess from her lips and chin. The tip of her soft-tongue, gently, grazing, Kami's face, as it creates a separation.

Kat's gaze was lasciviously – imperturbable; as she watches the Queens'. Kami exhales loudly: "Oh my goodness; I think –I just fell in love. Room for one more, perhaps?"; Kami says in a passively-sarcastic; yet seductive tone. Mona gives a sharp glare over at Kami, and grins a sinister grin: If looks could kill.

Kat rests on my lap, with her legs dangling over the arm of the chair. We find ourselves lying in bed, enjoying some of that magical sea breeze. We enjoy the rhythm composed by the waves; crashing against the starboard side of the ship. It actually has a very relaxing energy to it. I sat there listening to the waves for hours; as the Queens' slowly dozed off one-by-one. After a while, I found myself creeping out of bed; while trying to be as quiet as possible. I let the Queens' sleep; as I watched the sunrise. The morning rays are bouncing off the ocean. The waves weaving about the ocean reminds me of Kat's hair; flowing in the breeze. I allow myself to expand in the moment, taking it all in; as I close my eyes, and exhale; allowing the un-necessary to flow out.

REFLECTIONS

Today is our last day at sea: by morning we will have docked for the last time. When we first arrived on the ship, I overheard Kat telling Mona how great it would be to extend our vacation, after the cruise. Little do they know; I have one last surprise in store for my Queens.

I gaze into the mirror for a few, as I get ready for a Black-Tie, Event. "Daddy you are so sexy" Kat says to me while smiling. I smile back: almost bashful. Mona watches me get ready. She steps into the bathroom, and her hand slowly glides down my arm. "What cha doing?" – she says in a rather precariously-unpredictable tone. She also has that look in her eyes; as she sits on the counter, with her feet slightly swaying back and forth. Her legs slowly wrap themselves around my waist, and she locks her ankles; while using her powerful thighs to force me in closer. "You smell so good." – she says, as I feel her tongue sliding down my neck. She makes her way to my chest, leaving me amazed that she was able to avert my attention; as well as she did. I didn't even realize that my shirt had become unbuttoned… That's just how good; she truly is. Her tongue feels magnificent. She sucks on my nipples; which gets me every time.

I pull back and she quickly jumped off the counter, moving with me, and pulled my pants to the floor. She passionately shoves my dick into her mouth; so much so, that my knees instantly fall weak. Kat enters the bathroom. She paused, and a grin slowly covers her face. She watches for a bit; while leaning against the bathroom door.

I feel her hands start to move, as they rub across my back. She reaches around me, and grabs Mona by the hair; forcing me deeper and making her gag. Once again, the vibrations are so intense… Warm saliva runs rampant; flowing like hot lava. Her tongue cuffs so gently, leaving me unsure as to how much more I can take; as I grab the sides of the sink. Mona refuses to pull back… 'Good girl – that's right. Take it: take it all in…' I murmur. Kat gently pulls Mona's head back, and kisses her roughly and passionately. Kat takes ahold of Mona's hands, and holds them behind her back with one hand, while holding her hair in the other.

Now both ladies on their knees; as I'm about to erupt… Mona smiles while swallowing and making a slight "gulp," sound. I love it, and so does Kat – who's decided to join in. Both my Queens' now sliding up and down each side of me like a ride at the fair: allowing their tongues to set the stage. Kat focuses on the head while Mona stays closer to the balls. The sensations are driving me mad, and my body begins to do that thing that it does, and tingles. The Queens can tell; that this was nothing but pure pleasure for me. I feel the buildup, and I'm unsure as to how long I can hold it. Mona sees that I'm holding out; as she looks over at Kat. Together, they make it impossible for me, and moments later I shower them both: evening gowns and all.

Kat pulls back so that they both can experience the intense love storm. I lift them from the floor and wipe their faces, prior to preparing their shower and bath. I add bubbles to the bath, and salt crystals; with a touch of lavender to the shower. The steam from the shower quickly permeates the air, turning the room into a field of lavender flowers. Kat steps into the bath with sedulous care, and my assistance. She lays back and closes her eyes as the hot water takes over.

I place Mona into the shower and sit her down on the bench. I watch as the water hits the top of her head and flows down her face to the base of her neck; finding the perfect path to her breast and onto her nipples, where the water drips and pools in a puddle – that's collecting at the base of the shower. I turn and check on Kat one last time. Lips so soft, she raises up from her relaxing pose, for another kiss. I bend down to kiss her and next thing you know; I'm soaking wet.

Mona "laughs out loud" – thinking that it was just the funniest thing ever. Soaked from head-to-toe, and attire completely done for: I laugh along with the Queens'; simply living in the moment. Something tells me that this was their plan all along; just to keep from having to leave the room tonight. I must admit: I'm not complaining at all... I'll take my Queens' being happy over anything else; any-day. If the Queens' want to stay in for the rest of the night, then so be it.

I let Henry know that we will be staying in tonight. "No problem sir." Henry responds with what appears to be a bit of relief. "I think you'll have a much better time here, with the Ladies; sir." – Henry says; as he walks behind the bar and swiftly, picks-up the phone. Moments later the doorbell rings. A waitress arrives with menus and a round of cocktails. 'Mojitos: my favorite.' I say with relief. I see Kat and Mona peaking around the corner; out of my peripheral. They look sneaky and up to something; which is starting to become the norm for these two. They walk in with a little sass in their stride, smelling of both: confidence and corruption. We go over the menu and place our orders. The waitress leaves; to later return with our meals. Since it was our last night on the ship; I thought it appropriate, that Henry joined us for dinner. Darian came down from his suite, and joined us as well. We laughed and ate; as Henry told us stories about previous experiences, and Darian shared his adventures. Bottle-after-bottle; we drank: until the wee hours.

PERSEVERANCE

I awake to the ships horn: this is one hell of a crick I have in my neck. 'I guess last night will be forever memorable.' I say – as I struggle to rub it out, while scanning the room. I quickly attempt to regain my bearings after the horn almost gave me a heart attack; sounding again: indicating the final dock of our trip. Everyone seems to be suffering from last night ordeal. Kat and Mona had the couch completely covered. I look around to find Darian; who thought it'd be a great idea, to sleep in the Baby Grand Piano. 'I'm quite sure that's going to cost me.' I think to myself – as I attempt to get off of the floor. 'I'll have Lilly start the paperwork.' – I think out-loud.

'Speaking of… Where is Henry?' I ask. He is usual here with breakfast around this time; but not yet this morning. No omelet to devour, no mimosa to savor, no fresh fruit to jolt me awake. I walk out onto the balcony, and just as I begin to give my body that morning-stretch that it craves; I see Henry standing there; off to the side with breakfast for everyone. 'The heat is unbearable today: I could wake up to this kind of warmth more often; though, I hate that Kat made me cancel my deals.' – I think to myself. After a while, everyone starts to move around. I pass Kat and Mona a glass of Kat's, "secret remedy"; that Henry managed to whip up this morning. I'm still not sure how he understood anything that she was saying last evening; let alone, how he found all of her ingredients – while on a cruise ship. Good news is that everyone should be feeling better in roughly; twenty-minutes or so: It does actually work...

"Pling, plang, plong": echo's the sound of the keys; as Darian begins to crawl out of the piano: Head first onto the floor he goes. 'I really hope that he's okay.' – I say out loud. He manages to make it to his feet; but before he or anyone could say anything, or even comprehend what had just happened; with adrenaline filled excitement; Darian yells: "I'm good bitches;" and walks off – while tripping over items that were laying on the floor. I just look and shake my head in astonishment. I'm honestly not sure what I should say; so – this is all that I can do.

Amidst the chaos; the ladies have no choice but to sit up. " There's breakfast on the balcony ladies"; Henry advises. My beautiful Queens' exit the suite, onto the balcony where breakfast awaits.

We enjoy our last breakfast together; before leaving our tri-cation behind. Although more quiet than normal this morning; the Queens' share their thoughts, as to what they enjoyed most about the tri-cation. Henry walks back onto the balcony, where were seated and announces: "I just called for concierge to come and get your bags, sir." – prior to exiting the balcony. That was my queue. I remove my napkin from my lap; as I stand: I clear my throat. 'My extraordinary Queens'… I have a little surprise for you; My Loves…' – I say; as I whip out, what looks like more itineraries. I hand them each an envelope and watch with anticipation as they opened them. 'An 'extend-cation'; I explain as they simultaneously read from their envelopes. The Queens' looked at each other and their eyes buck and fill with excitement.

'Yes, Hawaii is our next destination.' I exclaimed!

Before they could say anything, I inform them that: I have taken care of everything, and that; my team has made the necessary arrangements, required to pull this extended vacation off. I kiss them both, and extend my hand out; guiding them into the suite, so that they could clean up and get ready to travel… Henry closes the suite door behind us and leads the way once again. We make our final walk; out of the private exit, and back onto dry land. Kat looks at me with those beautiful smiling eyes; as the car approaches. "A stretch Range Rover – huh?" she asks with a bit of sarcasm and glee. I smile and kiss her on the hand. Henry opens the door and we enter the car. We say our goodbyes; as Henry closes the door behind us.

ABOUT THE AUTHOR

Two simple people whose love has withstood some of the toughest of times. We've grown stronger with each test and we continue to nourish our gift into eternity. We simply want the world to be as happy as we are.

Wick'D Love